franny's feet™

The Lonely Library

By Kristin Ostby

Based on the television series *Franny's Feet*
created by Cathy Moss and Susin Nielsen

GROSSET & DUNLAP

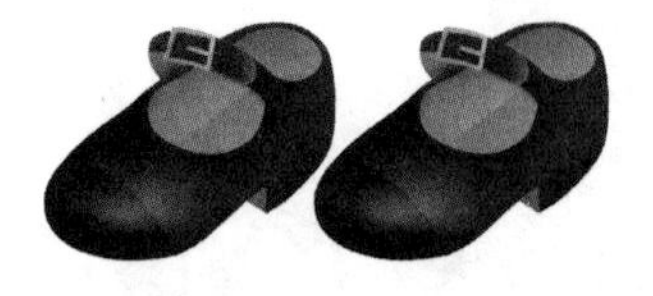

GROSSET & DUNLAP
Published by the Penguin Group
Penguin Group (USA) Inc., 375 Hudson Street, New York, New York 10014, USA
Penguin Group (Canada), 90 Eglinton Avenue East, Suite 700, Toronto, Ontario M4P 2Y3, Canada
(a division of Pearson Penguin Canada Inc.)
Penguin Books Ltd., 80 Strand, London WC2R 0RL, England
Penguin Group Ireland, 25 St. Stephen's Green, Dublin 2, Ireland
(a division of Penguin Books Ltd.)
Penguin Group (Australia), 250 Camberwell Road, Camberwell, Victoria 3124, Australia
(a division of Pearson Australia Group Pty. Ltd.)
Penguin Books India Pvt. Ltd., 11 Community Centre, Panchsheel Park, New Delhi—110 017, India
Penguin Group (NZ), 67 Apollo Drive, Rosedale, North Shore 0632, New Zealand
(a division of Pearson New Zealand Ltd.)
Penguin Books (South Africa) (Pty.) Ltd., 24 Sturdee Avenue,
Rosebank, Johannesburg 2196, South Africa

Penguin Books Ltd, Registered Offices:
80 Strand, London WC2R 0RL, England

Library of Congress Control Number: 2007034409

ISBN 978-0-448-44837-4 10 9 8 7 6 5 4 3 2 1

Franny Fantootsie loves to go to her grandfather's shoe repair shop. She always meets new people and goes on *frantastic* adventures.

One afternoon, Grandpa read aloud to Franny. "So the princess kissed the frog, and the frog turned into—"

"I know, I know!" interrupted Franny. "He turned into a slimy, green prince! Ew!"

Grandpa laughed. "That's right, Franny."

Just then, the bell on the shop door rang and a woman walked inside.

"A customer!" Franny cried.

"And what can we do for you?" Grandpa asked the woman.

"My work shoes are all worn-out," said the woman, "and I need good shoes since I walk around all day. I'm a librarian, you see."

"Oh, we love the library!" said Franny.

"We'll bring you your shoes when we return our books," said Grandpa.

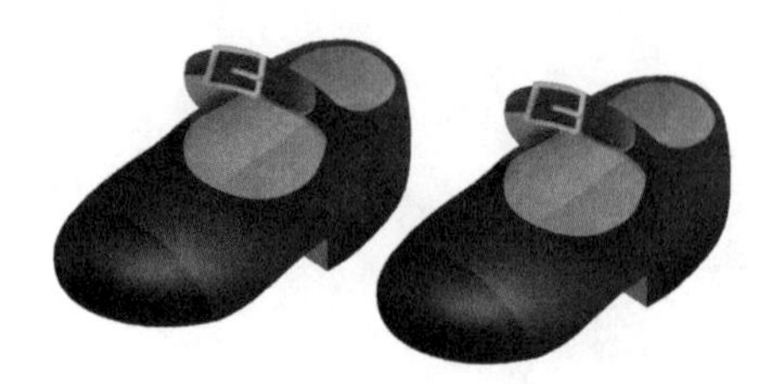

Grandpa handed the shoes to Franny.

"Into the fix-it box they go!" she said.

Franny placed the shoes beside the fix-it box. Then she carefully slid her feet inside them.

"Where will my feet take me today?" Franny asked.

And in a flash of stars, Franny was whisked to a faraway place.

Franny suddenly found herself in the biggest library she'd ever seen.

"Whoa!" she said. "There must be a million, trillion, gazillion books here!"

Franny pulled a book off the shelf. Then she sat down and looked at the beautiful pictures.

Just then, Franny heard a noise and looked up from her book.

"Anybody there?" she asked.

No one answered, but when she looked back down at her book, it was gone! The book was scuttling away all by itself!

"Wait a minute!" said Franny. "There's a tail underneath that book!"

When Franny caught up to her book, she picked it up to see who or what was underneath it.

"A mouse!" cried Franny.

"That's right!" said the mouse. "Now get out of here, you book stealer!"

"I'm not a book stealer!" said Franny. "I'm Franny, and I love books."

"No one loves books more than Henry," said the mouse. "That's me. Henry."

"Oh yeah?" said Franny. "How many books have you read?"

"Oh," said Henry. "I can't read—not a word. I just love looking at all the pictures and making up my own stories!"

Franny smiled. "Maybe a friend could read them to you, just like my grandpa does for me!"

"Friends?" said Henry. "I don't have time for *friends*."

"Well," Franny said hopefully, "maybe we could look at some pictures together. But not as friends, of course," she said with a grin.

Henry was so excited that he started running in circles. "There are a million, trillion, gazillion books for us to look at!" he said. "Come on!"

"Okay," said Franny. "But let's start with just one book and take it from there."

"There is one book I've always wanted to read," said Henry. "But it's around the corner near where Sally, a horrible, big-fanged library cat, lives."

"She can't be *that* scary," said Franny.

"Do the words 'saber-toothed tiger' mean anything to you?" asked Henry.

"Oh, phooey!" said Franny. "I'm not afraid." And with that, Franny went to find the book.

As Franny turned a corner, she heard a scary-sounding voice: "What big teeth you have," it said. "The better to eat you with my child . . ."

"Ahhh!" screamed Franny as she started to run away. "The saber-toothed tiger!"

Just then, the scary voice changed. "A saber-toothed tiger? Where? Sally isn't afraid of you . . ."

Franny stopped in her tracks. When she turned around, she saw a cute orange cat. "You're Sally?" she asked.

"Yes," said Sally. "And there's a saber-toothed tiger around here, so I'd better protect you."

"But *you're* the saber-toothed tiger," said Franny.

"Me?" asked Sally. "Nah. I'm just a library cat who spends her days reading books to . . . well, to other books." Sally sighed. "I don't have any friends."

That gave Franny an idea. "Stay right here," she said to Sally.

She raced back to Henry and grabbed him by the hand. "Come on!" she said. "I want you to meet someone very special."

"Not *you*!" cried Sally and Henry when they came face-to-face.

"Come on, Franny," said Henry. "Let's leave this book-stealer alone."

"But she's *my* friend, too," said Sally. "Right, Franny?"

"You know," said Franny, "you two have so much in common. Have you ever tried talking to each other?"

"No," said Sally. "Why would I want to?"

"Never," said Henry. "I repeat, *never*."

"Well," Franny said with a sigh, "I'll just have to get that book from the top shelf by myself."

"*That* shelf?" asked Henry.

"But I've always wanted to read that book!" said Sally.

"*You* like books?" Sally and Henry asked each other at the same time.

"Yes," said Henry. "But I can't read. I just make up stories to go with the pictures. Can you read?"

"That's pretty much all I do every day," said Sally.

"Guys!" hollered Franny. "I could use some help!"

"I'll help you on this side," said Sally.

"And I'll help you on this side," said Henry.

"Got it!" said Franny as she grabbed the book.

Sally and Henry sat down to look at the book.

"I can't wait to teach you to read," said Sally.

"And I can't wait for you to read to me, best friend," said Henry.

"Friend?" asked Sally. "I thought you didn't want any friends."

"I was just waiting for my best friend to come along," Henry said. "And that's you!"

"I think that's what I was waiting for, too!" said Sally.

"Thanks for introducing us, Franny," Sally and Henry said at the same time.

"You're welcome!" Franny said. "I have to get back to my Grandpa now! Have fun reading!"

"Bye, Franny!" they said.

Franny landed back at the shoe shop as quickly as she'd left it. "That was *frantastic*!" she said. She slipped the librarian's shoes off and tossed them into the fix-it box.

A blue bookmark fluttered out of one of the shoes. "A bookmark!" Franny smiled. "Another treasure for my shoebox," she said, gently placing it inside.

A moment later, Franny found Grandpa snoozing in his chair.
"Grandpa?" Franny whispered.
Grandpa opened his eyes. "Yes, muffin?"
"Will you always read to me, even after I've learned to read for myself, just like Sally Cat and Henry Mouse?"

Grandpa chuckled. "I don't know who Sally and Henry are, but I will always read to you," he said. "In fact, why don't I read you a story right now? How about this one?"

"That's a good one!" Franny answered.

Franny went on a wonderful adventure today, and another one is just around the corner. "Where will my feet take me tomorrow?"